OTHER YOUNG YEARLING BOOKS
YOU WILL ENJOY:

YEARLING BOOKS/YOUNG YEARLINGS/YEARLING CLASSICS are designed especially to entertain and enlighten young people. Patricia Reilly Giff, consultant to this series, received her bachelor's degree from Marymount College and a master's degree in history from St. John's University. She holds a Professional Diploma in Reading and a Doctorate of Humane Letters from Hofstra University. She was a teacher and reading consultant for many years, and is the author of numerous books for young readers.

For a complete listing of all Yearling titles, write to
Dell Readers Service,
P.O. Box 1045,
South Holland, IL 60473.

LITTLE SOUP'S TURKEY

Robert Newton Peck

Illustrated by Charles Robinson

A YOUNG YEARLING BOOK

Published by
Dell Publishing
a division of
Bantam Doubleday Dell Publishing Group, Inc.
666 Fifth Avenue
New York, New York 10103

The trademark Yearling® is registered in the U.S. Patent and Trademark Office.

The trademark Dell® is registered in the U.S. Patent and Trademark Office.

ISBN: 0-440-40724-9

Printed in the United States of America

November 1992

10   9   8   7   6   5   4   3   2   1

CWO

*This book is dedicated
to every adult who
has read a book to a kid.*

LITTLE SOUP'S TURKEY

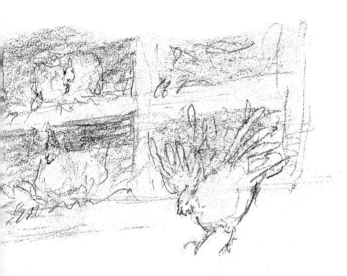

One

Howdy.
What's your name?
I am Robert Newton Peck.

How old am I?

Well, I'm about your age.

Don't bother to call me Robert.

Papa calls me Robert whenever I am late to the barn for milking.

You can call me Rob.

Everybody does.

As you can guess, my family and I live on a farm.

Our farm is in Vermont.

What state do you live in?

Our farm is very small.

But I am a lot smaller.

Like you, I go to school too.

But I seldom go alone, or come home alone, because I have a pal.

A best pal.

Luther Wesley Vinson.

His nickname is Soup.

One Saturday morning, Soup was helping me clean out the henhouse.

It needed sweeping.

Chickens drop a lot more than eggs.

They lose feathers every day.

My job took about an hour.

However, with Soup to help me, it took two.

If my cousin, Ben Peck, had been there, it would have taken three hours.

Or perhaps forever.

My father's rule was simple, when boys were helping him with his farming:

"One boy," Papa said, "is worth one boy. Two boys are half a boy. And three boys are no boy at all."

We finally got finished.

Soup smelled worse than a chicken, and so did I.

This was okay by me.

After milking, I smelled like a cow.

On Saturday night, I smelled of soap.

"Rob," said Soup, "let's go to my house."

So we did.

It wasn't very far.

We tossed pebbles for a bit, pretending they were real agate marbles.

Then we put a saddle on Soup's dog.

That lasted for about five minutes,

until the dog got tired of the game, bit us, and ran away.

Saddle and all.

"Look," said Soup.

He pointed.

I looked.

"Here comes Pa in his wagon," Soup said.

We went to meet him.

Mr. Vinson, in a way, was a lot like *my* father.

Neither man wasted much of the day on either talking or smiling.

The wagon stopped.

Behind Mr. Vinson, in the long

wagon bin, there was a large wooden crate.

Something moved inside.

An animal.

Two

"Rob," said Soup, "it's a turkey."
He was right.
We climbed over the tailgate,

up into the wagon, to take a close look.

Sure enough, inside the crate was a turkey.

It was a male turkey, a gobbler.

He was very very large.

This gobbler was the biggest turkey that I had ever seen.

"Wow," said Soup.

"I wonder how much he weighs," I said.

"My guess," Soup said, "would be close to forty pounds. Maybe more."

He was almost too big for the crate.

Standing there, I was wondering how Soup's father, Mr. Vinson, could lift the crate off the wagon.

He handled the job easily. By not doing it.

All he did was pry a few wooden slats loose with a claw hammer.

The nails squeaked as they popped loose.

They also bent.

And then . . . *surprise!*

That old tom turkey scooted from his crate faster than a bullet leaves a gun.

Well, almost as fast.

He jumped off the wagon.

Soup and I jumped off too.

"Hold it," Soup told me.

"What's the matter?"

"We're not supposed to chase after the turkey," Soup said.

So we didn't.

But we still had fun.

Soup and I pretended to be spies. We ran around the barn. Then, on tiptoe, we sneaked up behind some bushes to spy on Soup's turkey.

We didn't get very close.

Somehow, that old turkey gobbler seemed to know exactly where Soup and I were.

He either heard us or smelled us.

"Soup," I said, "I wonder if I smell good-to-eat to a turkey."

Soup took a quick sniff of me. Then he made a face.

"You don't smell very good to me."

"I don't?"

"Rob, if you were a dog, you wouldn't even smell good-to-eat to a flea."

"How do I smell?" I asked Soup.

"With your nose." He laughed.

It was great having Soup for a pal.

I laughed too.

Three

Miss Kelly was smiling.

Whenever our teacher smiled, she had a way of making a cloudy day shine.

"I have an idea," Miss Kelly said.

Soup leaned closer to my right ear.

"If it's homework," he said, "don't count me to be in favor of it."

Luckily, it wasn't about homework.

"As you all know," Miss Kelly said, "we are now in the month of . . ."

"November," we all said.

"Correct. And the month of November has a very special holiday for everyone here in America."

"Thanksgiving," we said.

Miss Kelly nodded.

"So," she said, "I think it might be

fun to invite all of your mothers and fathers to our school."

"To eat?" asked Soup.

"To see," she told us, "our very special Thanksgiving play."

Soup and I looked at each other.

Neither of us had ever been in a play before, and the idea was bigger than I could imagine.

Norma Jean Bissell raised her hand.

I saw her do it.

In fact, whenever we were all in school, I noticed *everything* Norma Jean did.

Miss Kelly looked at her.

"Yes?" she responded.

"Who'll be *in* the play?" Norma Jean asked.

"All of you," Miss Kelly told us.

Inside, I had always wanted to act in a play.

But I never told anyone about it.

Not even Soup.

"Our play," said Miss Kelly, "will be about the Pilgrims, who wanted to give thanks."

"What did they do?" I asked.

"They invited the Indians to a feast."

"Where," asked Soup, "will we act out a play?"

"Here," said Miss Kelly.

"Here?" I asked.

"Yes. We can stretch a length of clothesline from one wall, up front, to the other."

"What for?"

"To hang two bedsheets on," Miss Kelly said, "to use as our curtain."

I smiled.

A play sounded like fun.

"And," said Miss Kelly, "we can discover how the early Pilgrims learned to plant *corn.*"

We lived on a farm.

My father planted corn every spring.

So I thought that *everyone* knew all about corn planting. It was easy.

But no good farmer ever planted corn in the same ground two seasons in a row.

Corn takes too much out of the soil.

So, in between, we raised alfalfa.

Do you know what alfalfa is used for?

It's silage. To feed cows.

Corn grows tall.

Alfalfa spreads short and green.

Sometimes, in an alfalfa field, a few cornstalks stick up high.

One here, another over there.
This is corn that wasn't planted.
Papa had a name for it.
Volunteer corn.

Four

"Corn," said Soup.

The two of us were standing in a barn.

It was Soup's barn.

Not mine.

All around us, we could see tall shocks of corn, brought in at harvest time.

"Ah," said Soup, "Miss Kelly said we'll need plenty of corn for the play."

"Here it is," I said.

Now, if Soup's family didn't have enough corn, I knew that I could borrow some from my father.

If he wasn't watching.

"We harvested three kinds of corn," said Soup.

"What are they?"

Soup said, "One is field corn. For fodder. It's silo corn for cows. Another kind is sweet corn, to eat."

"What was the third kind?"

"I forgot," Soup said.

We started to collect the corn.

Not in shocks.

Not in ears.

In kernels.

Miss Kelly had told us that we would need a whole lot of corn.

For our stage.

"Why?" we had asked her.

"So," she said, "the Pilgrims can be thankful for a bountiful harvest."

"Rob," said Soup, "we need a bag."
"Why?"
"To hold all the corn."
We found one.

It was easy to find a bag.
Yet it wasn't so easy to shuck all of the corn kernels off the ears, and into the bag.
This chore really took time.
Plenty of it.
But we finally completed our corn job.

Ear after ear we shucked into the burlap bag.

Kernel by kernel it filled.

Soup sighed.

"Rob," he said, "finished at last."

"Thank the giving," I said.

"Now," said Soup, "all we have left to do is carry all these kernels of raw corn to our school."

"Maybe," I said, "Papa can help."

My father met Miss Kelly once.

We met her on the street, in town.

"Papa," I said, "here comes my teacher."

"Miss Kelly?" he'd asked me.

"Yes," I said. "Here she comes."

That was when I saw my father, a man who could neither read nor write, take off his hat. In respect to a teacher.

"Miss Kelly," I said, "this is my father. He kills hogs."

"Mr. Peck," my teacher said, offering Papa her hand, "I'm so grateful that you sent Robert to our school."

Papa didn't say anything.

Not at first.

He just shifted his weight, from one big dirty boot to another, as if not knowing what to say.

Or do.

He held his hat in his hand.

"Whatever he breaks," he said, "I'll pay for."

Five

We wrote the play ourselves.
Miss Kelly helped.
Our play was about the Pilgrims

and Indians and their first Thanksgiving.

We had twenty-eight kids in our school.

"We'll have fourteen Pilgrims," said Miss Kelly, "and fourteen Indians."

Soup was a Pilgrim.

But I was an Indian.

"Miss Kelly," I said, "I want to be a Pilgrim, like Soup."

Miss Kelly sighed.

She was on her knees, trying to fit a gray Pilgrim dress on Norma Jean Bissell.

"*You,*" she told me, "are an Indian, and that is all there is to it."

I didn't argue.

The *real* reason I wanted to be a Pilgrim wasn't because Soup got to be one.

If I were a Pilgrim, then I'd get to stand next to Norma Jean.

That, I was thinking, would make me feel quite thankful.

Boys who were Pilgrims got to do something special.

They held guns.

But not real guns.

Merely toys.

Soup made his own gun.

Its long barrel was a broomstick.

The front end was a funnel, because a Pilgrim gun looks a lot like a slide trombone.

The shoulder stock was an old roof shingle, shaped like a skinny triangle.

Soup painted his gun black.

Because I was going to be an Indian, I needed a bow and arrow.

So I made them myself.

The bow was easy.

It was just a yardstick bent into a

slight curve, held in that position by a length of thick twine.

Twine is string.

Making my arrow was harder.

It was a straight shaft of wood.

An arrow has something at both ends.

In front, I folded the lid from a tin can into a tiny, shiny triangle.

That's called an arrowhead.

In back, I stuck on a few chicken feathers.

Earlier, I planned to use tail feathers from Soup's turkey.

But he (the turkey) didn't seem to appear as if he'd let me pull a few out.

So I turned chicken, you might say.

At last my arrow was ready.

Something in front, and something in the rear.

Like a *cigar*.

Papa smoked a cigar once.

Somebody had given it to him.

It made the kitchen half smoke and half smell.

Mama opened the kitchen door and left it open, to air out.

Later, but loud enough for Papa to hear, she told me what a *cigar* was.

"A flame in front," Mama said, "and a fool in back."

Papa almost smiled.

Six

We collected more corn.

I knew there were three kinds of corn.

Field corn, for cows.

Sweet corn, for people.

And a third kind that I couldn't quite remember.

Maybe it was my father's *seed corn,* which was very important to save in a dry place.

Soup and I hit a bit of trouble.

That big old tom turkey kept wanting to eat up all the kernels of corn.

We were planning to take the corn to school. For our play.

It wasn't easy to battle a turkey.

Soup's father told us that the big turkey weighed close to fifty pounds.

We called him Terrible Tom.

So Soup and I cooked up a Thanksgiving joke as part of our play.

Miss Kelly approved.

"A turkey joke," she told Soup and me, "is just perfect for Thanksgiving."

I was hoping for warm weather on the day that we were performing the play for our parents.

This, I knew, wasn't too hopeful.

In northern Vermont, at the end of November, the weather isn't much like noon in June.

The Pilgrims, however, would keep warm.

Pilgrim girls would be wearing long gray dresses.

Pilgrim boys had knickers, long

clawhammer coats, shoes with buckles, and wool stockings.

Both wore large white collars.

Miss Kelly let the Pilgrim kids cut their collars out of white cardboard.

The rest of us, we who were the Indians, wore next to nothing.

We weren't naked, but only a thread away.

Mr. Graziano of Graziano's Grocery donated our Indian makeup.

It came in a large metal drum.

Not the kind of a drum that's in a band and is played with drumsticks.

This drum was a container.

Inside, we discovered, were pounds and pounds of powder.

The powder was a reddy-brown.

"Cocoa," said Miss Kelly.

"How does it work?" asked one of our Indians.

Before I could say *how*, Miss Kelly stripped off my shirt and sweater.

Then she rubbed cocoa all over my arms, chest, face, neck, hands, and back.

I looked in our old cracked mirror.

But I didn't see Rob Peck.

I saw red.

Seven

We had to practice our play.
Part of the play was dancing.
"Pilgrims," said Miss Kelly, "didn't
dance."

Indians did.

Our fourteen Indians were divided into two groups.

Seven each.

Dancers and drummers.

Miss Kelly brought seven old hat-boxes to school.

They were all shaped like a circle or an oval.

We painted them bright colors.

For drumsticks, we padded the heads of long wooden cooking spoons.

The drums really sounded Indian.

BOOM . . . boom . . . boom . . . boom. BOOM . . . boom . . . boom

. . . boom. BOOM . . . boom . . .
boom . . . boom.

"Miss Kelly," I asked, "do I get to
be one of the drummers?"

"No," she said. "Robert, you're a
born dancer."

"Why?"

"Because you so rarely sit still."

That settled that!

Maybe, however, my wild Indian
dancing would capture the eye (or the
heart) of a certain Pilgrim.

Norma Jean Bissell.

So I practiced my Indian dancing at every spare minute.

In the pasture, I danced for our cows.

None of them seemed to notice.

Not even one cow clapped.

They only chewed.

Beyond the cow barn, I danced in the pigpen for our pig.

He didn't notice either.

In the hen yard, I tried dancing for the chickens.

The hens looked at me as if my brain weren't plugged in.

Our animals, one by one, were making me wonder if my fancy dance steps could impress Norma Jean.

I was the only Indian dancer who really let loose, war-whooping as I kicked up the dust.

Miss Kelly admitted that what I lacked in talent I made up in noise.

At least I made the Pilgrims laugh.

"That," said our teacher, "wasn't easy."

Eight

We brought the corn to school.

"My," said Miss Kelly, "I never knew there was so much extra corn in Vermont."

She looked very pleased, because we'd brought seven bags of corn.

"Our costumes are ready," Miss Kelly said. "And so are the bows, arrows, and guns. We need only one more thing."

Soup and I asked her what it was.

Miss Kelly smiled. "A turkey."

Soup winked at me.

Then, to our teacher, he said, "Rob and I will take care of that."

I blinked.

"We will?"

"Right," said Soup.

Some of the kids in our play were given names.

But very few.

Soup was Captain Myles Standish.

"Miss Kelly," I said, "I want to be a captain too."

She sighed.

"Indians didn't have captains, Robert."

"How about if I'm a general?"

"They didn't have *those* either."

"Well, I ought to have some sort of a *name*."

Miss Kelly raised an eyebrow.

"A name?"

"Yes, you know . . . like Sitting Bull or Sitting Duck or something important."

"Ah," said Miss Kelly. She snapped her fingers. "I have an idea, Robert."

"For my name?"

"Yes."

"What is it?"

"You can be . . . Squanto."

"Is he a captain?"

"Well, not exactly. But he was more important than a captain or a general."

"Honest?"

Miss Kelly nodded.

"Was this Squat guy a—?"

"No, not Squat—his name was Squanto."

"Was he as big as Soup?"

Miss Kelly glanced over to where Soup was explaining musket fire to several of the Pilgrim girls.

"No one," she said, "is as big as Soup in his Pilgrim britches."

* * *

"What did Squanto do?" I asked.

"Something very important. In fact," said Miss Kelly, "it was a most useful gift to the Pilgrims."

"Gunpowder?"

"No, not gunpowder. There's more to enjoying life than just shooting a musket."

"Like what?"

"Corn."

Nine

It was Wednesday.
The big day finally came.
Play day.

Soup and I brought Terrible Tom to school.

This wasn't easy.

He didn't want to go.

"Goodness," said Miss Kelly, "I had no idea your turkey would be so . . . so *big.*"

We strung up a clothesline.

On it, we hung the bedsheets.

Our curtain was ready.

All we needed now was an audience of mothers and fathers.

They finally came.

As I had feared, the weather turned cold.

Shivering, I smeared on an extra coat of cocoa. To keep warm.

Then another.

We Indians huddled backstage, behind the curtain, as close as possible to the big black stove.

It was very hot.

Out in front, Soup and the other Pilgrims were explaining their feast preparations to the audience.

"This," said Norma Jean, "is hominy."

"It's something," said Soup, "like a melody."

Nobody laughed.

"Here come the Indians," said Norma Jean.

Nothing happened.

We Indians were too cold to leave the stove.

There we herded, with all our corn and hatbox drums.

"I *said*, here come the Indians *now!*" repeated Norma Jean.

We didn't budge.

"*Now,*" snapped Miss Kelly.

It was time for my dance.

The drummers all thumped their hatboxes.

BOOM . . . boom . . . boom . . . boom.

I danced, because I was freezing to death.

But I danced around like a crazy person, until something fell backstage.

KA-BANG-BOOM.

I couldn't see what it was.

It sounded heavy, like all seven bags of our corn.

I didn't know what to do next.

All I could remember was that I was supposed to tell Norma Jean Bissell who I was.

There stood Norma Jean, waiting.

"My . . . name is . . . is . . ."

I couldn't recall my name.

Leaning close to my ear, Norma Jean whispered to me, to remind me what to say.

I smiled at the audience.

"My name," I said, "is Squanto, you turkey."

For some reason, all the grown-ups laughed, except for Miss Kelly, who sort of winced.

"Squanto," said Norma Jean, "did you bring us a turkey?"

"Yes," I said, still dancing my heart out and my cocoa off. "And I'll also teach you Pilgrims how to . . . how to . . ."

"Plant corn," Miss Kelly whispered.

"Plant corn," I repeated.

My mother and Aunt Carrie looked relieved, and almost proud.

"Bring the corn," I said.

Nobody did anything.

"Bring the corn *now*," ordered Miss Kelly.

I heard one cold Indian chatter, "We can't."

"Why not?"

"Because Rob's dancing knocked the corn too near the stove. And the corn is—is *burning*."

Ten

Pop!

I heard a noise coming from back-stage.

Then more noises.

Pop! Pop! Pop!

Then a lot of *pops*. Not just a dozen, or a hundred.

I heard thousands.

Pop! Pop! Poppety-pop-pop-pop-pop . . .

Too late, I now remembered.

Soup and I had brought the third kind of corn. The mystery kind.

Popcorn!

And lots of it.

Seven bags.

Before it pops, popcorn is very small.

But once it pops, it becomes ten or twenty times larger.

It sure scared Tom.

No one had to say "Bring the turkey."

Out from behind the curtain charged Terrible Tom, with fear in both eyes.

He came very fast, squawking, and with his big wings flapping.

The audience looked very surprised.

The curtain fell.

By accident.

Several of the Pilgrim kids (the ones that had to eat hominy) threw up.

An Indian stepped on his hatbox drum, busted it badly, and cried.

Some of the Indians kept warm by hitting the Pilgrims with their drumsticks.

Twenty-eight kids, one wild turkey, and a ton of popcorn seemed to be flying everywhere.

Everybody bumped into everybody else.

Suddenly there seemed to be more cocoa on the Pilgrims than on the Indians.

Mothers screamed, and fathers fainted.

*　*　*

Miss Kelly considered retirement.

"Soup and Rob," she yelled at us, "catch Terrible Tom, and tell your turkey joke."

"Now?" we asked.

"Yes," pleaded our teacher. *"Now."*

We caught Terrible Tom with a cowboy lasso and a flying tackle.

"Here's our joke," said Soup to the audience.

"Where does a fifty-pound turkey go?" I asked.

Soup laughed. "Anywhere he wants to!"

* * *

The play ended.

We were all very thankful to be alive, and Miss Kelly seemed the most thankful.

Some mothers brought cookies.

Fathers brought jugs of sweet apple cider.

And there was popcorn for everyone.

We had a party. And a prayer.

Miss Kelly spat out a turkey feather, smiled, and said how thankful she was to be our teacher.

I threw a handful of cocoa powder at Soup, and he bopped me over the head with a hatbox.

Four times.

It sounded both funny and familiar.

Boom . . . boom . . . boom . . . boom.